ENIGMA
A MAGICAL MYSTERY
Graeme Base

Abrams Books for Young Readers
New York

YOUNG Bertie Badger's Grandpa was a conjurer of note,
With magic spells and magic wand and magic hat and coat.
A Master of Illusion, an Ambassador of Fate,
The famous, one and only, world-renowned Gadzooks the Great.

From London to the Spanish Steps, from Prague to Kathmandu,
Then on to the Antipodes and back through Timbuktu,
For fifty years he'd wowed the crowds and roundly been admired,
But now he lived a quiet life—Gadzooks the Great (Retired).

His magic wand lay idle on the bookshelf by the door,
His hat and cape beside it, neither worn much anymore.
For nowadays old Grandpa's tricks were saved for one alone:
The grandson he adored so much, young Bertie Badgerstone.

But on the days that Bertie came, the shadows leaped and twirled,
And Grandpa Badger's living room became a different world.
Gadzooks the Great was back again, and Bertie clapped and cheered,
As charms were laid and spells were cast and rabbits disappeared.

One day, when Bertie came along to watch the magic show,
He found old Grandpa waiting with a tale of grief and woe.
"It looks as though our little show cannot go on," he said.
"For someone has been up to tricks . . ." He sadly shook his head.

It seemed that all the residents had woken up that day
To find their special magic props had somehow gone astray.
"My top hat, cape, and wand have gone, but there is worse to tell:
My precious magic bunny rabbit's disappeared as well!"

"Don't worry," Bertie said at once. "I'll solve this, have no fear,
For magic things that vanish almost always reappear.
Until I find them, every one, I swear I shall not rest."
Then Bertie hugged his Grandpa and set off upon his quest.

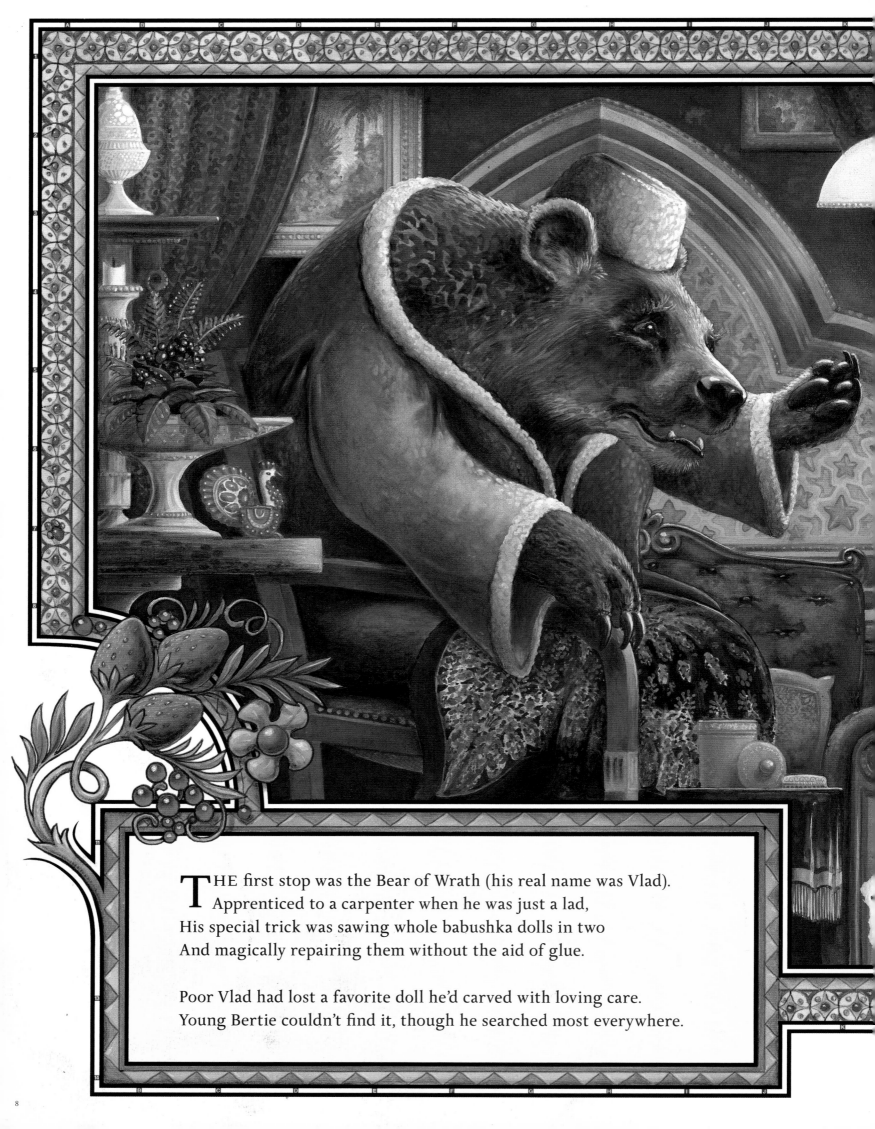

THE first stop was the Bear of Wrath (his real name was Vlad).
Apprenticed to a carpenter when he was just a lad,
His special trick was sawing whole babushka dolls in two
And magically repairing them without the aid of glue.

Poor Vlad had lost a favorite doll he'd carved with loving care.
Young Bertie couldn't find it, though he searched most everywhere.

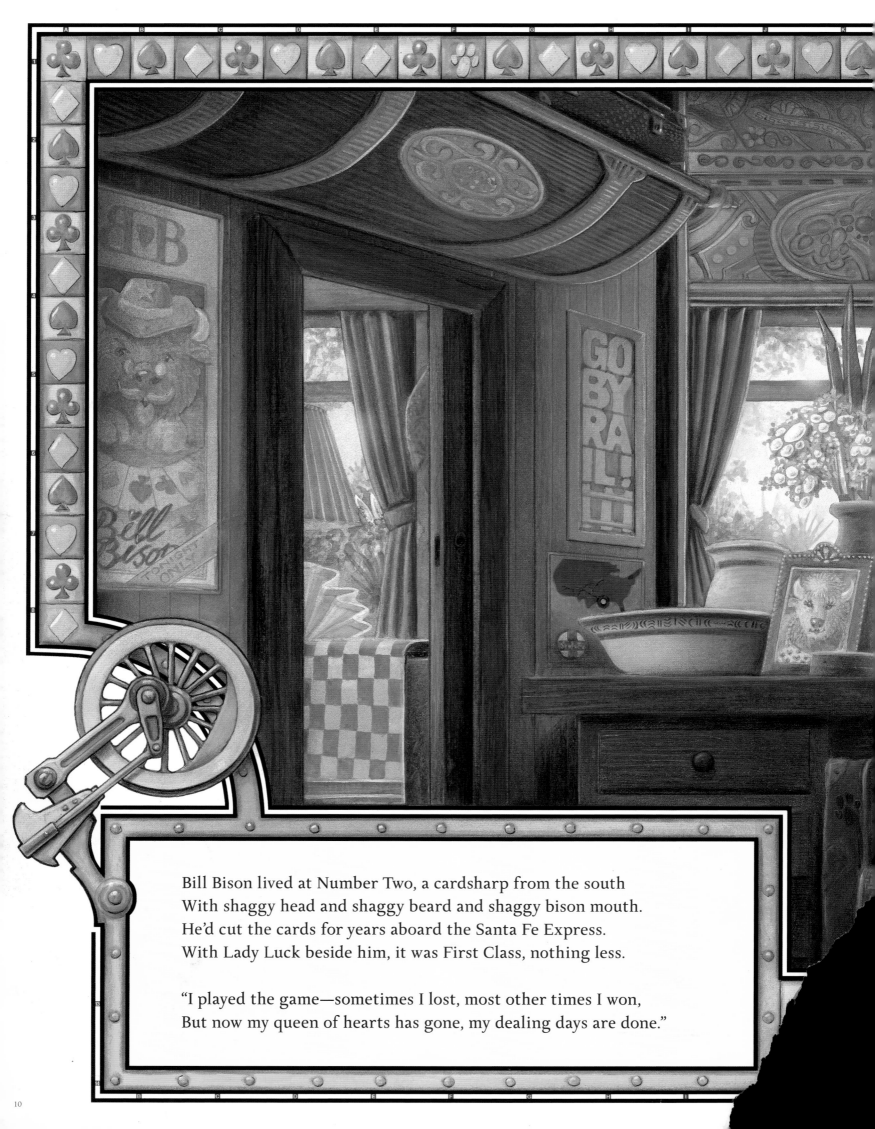

Bill Bison lived at Number Two, a cardsharp from the south
With shaggy head and shaggy beard and shaggy bison mouth.
He'd cut the cards for years aboard the Santa Fe Express.
With Lady Luck beside him, it was First Class, nothing less.

"I played the game—sometimes I lost, most other times I won,
But now my queen of hearts has gone, my dealing days are done."

The next stop was the Monkey House. Young Bertie ventured in
And all at once felt giddy as his head began to spin.
Three cheeky rascals, experts on the jungle-gym trapeze,
Swung wildly through the vines that hung in loops from all the trees.

The monkeys' trick involved a set of interlocking rings,
But these were marked as "missing" on the list of magic things.

Now Bertie knocked at Number Four . . . but silence reigned supreme.
The door swung open soundlessly, as if it were a dream,
For this was where Miss Poodle lived, the Mademoiselle of Mime,
And for an hour, without a sound, she acted out the crime.

Though Bertie thought she'd lost her voice (why else the long charade?),
It turned out that her ball and cups had somehow been mislaid.

Miss Pollyanna Parropoup, the Goddess of Caracas,
Was nothing if not colorful—she even played maracas!
She'd wowed the Venezuelan Club some thirty years ago,
Where every night her plumage and percussion stole the show.

Her trick was reading minds, but now her own had gone astray—
"Poor Polly's lost her crackers!" was the only thing she'd say.

Room Six belonged to Hoo Min Floo, Lord Pandamonium,
Who'd picked up levitation from his Flying Panda mum.
He once had raised the Chinese Wall—a miracle—but then
He dropped it on the Emperor's foot, and never worked again.

His power came from three jade bells he kept beneath his gown,
But now that they were missing, all his spells came crashing down.

Room Seven was a chamber filled with incense and perfume,
Adorned with rugs and swathes of silk that swept across the room.
And here Mistress Hypnosis wove her ancient magic spell,
Possessed of an enduring charm that time could not dispel.

Her powers of persuasion, once the wonder of the age,
Had failed her since her Mystic Sphinx of Sleep had been mislaid.

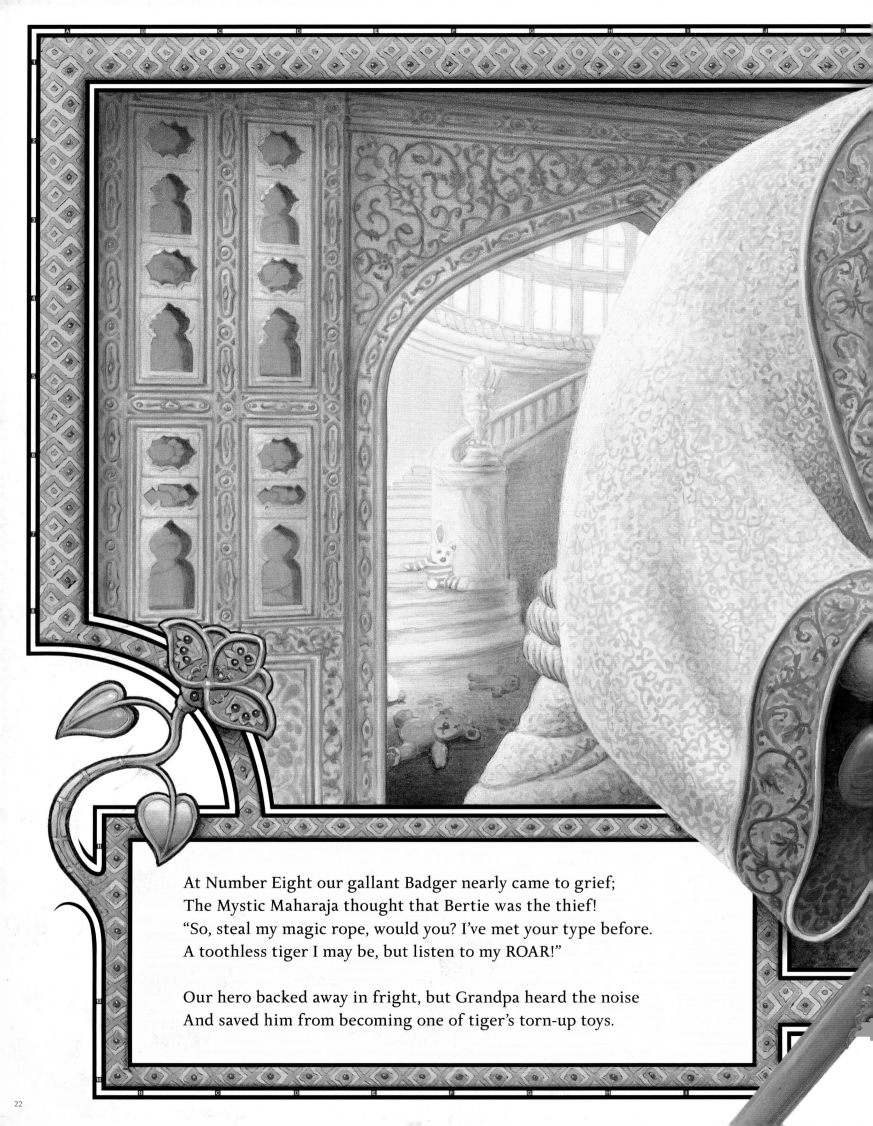

At Number Eight our gallant Badger nearly came to grief;
The Mystic Maharaja thought that Bertie was the thief!
"So, steal my magic rope, would you? I've met your type before.
A toothless tiger I may be, but listen to my ROAR!"

Our hero backed away in fright, but Grandpa heard the noise
And saved him from becoming one of tiger's torn-up toys.

POOR Bertie sat in Grandpa's room, the last one that was left,
And knew the magic show was doomed. He'd failed to solve the theft.
Old Grandpa sat there sadly. "How I miss my long-eared friend.
To think that after all these years our show is at an end.

"We toured the world, we hit the heights, old floppy ears and I.
A double act, a partnership . . ." He sighed a heartfelt sigh.
Then Bertie heard a snuffle, and a muffled voice that said,
"Don't cry," and Grandpa's rabbit crawled from underneath the bed!

"Enigma!" Grandpa cried with joy. "Enigma, is it you?
I thought that you were gone for good. I can't believe it's true!"
He held him close and cuddled him while Bertie gave a cheer.
"Now tell me all that happened—how you came to disappear."

But as old Grandpa looked at him with fondness and relief,
The rabbit hung his head in shame and whispered, "I'm the thief!"
The Badgers both were lost for words. "The thief? But how? But why?"
And so Enigma told them, with a sniffle and a sigh:

"For all my life I've been the one who jumped out of the hat.
I asked myself, 'Why always me? What's good and fair in that?'
Just once, before the curtain falls, could I not cast the spell?
And wear the magic hat and cape, and wave the wand as well?

"And so I took the magic things to help with my routine:
'The Most Amazing Rabbit That the World Has Ever Seen.'
But everything I borrowed has just vanished in thin air—
I hid them all so carefully, I can't remember where.

"I even wrote a list." He held a sheet for them to see.
"It's all in secret code—but now I can't recall the key!"

"Dear friend," said Grandpa kindly, "what you say is only right.
I've hogged the stage for long enough—it's time you had your night."
And Bertie added, "Goodness knows where all those things have gone,
But now we need replacements. There's a show that must go on!"

He opened up his schoolbag with a cheeky badger grin.
"This bag has special powers . . . who can say what lies within?
Behold! I've got a magic wand! Enchanted rope! Five rings!
There's everything we need—a brand-new set of magic things!"

"Gadzooks," cried Grandpa, "what a trick!" His voice rang down the hall.
"My clever grandson is the best magician of us all."

AND so the magic show was saved—in fact it hit new heights.
And all of Grandpa's friends joined in, a magic night of nights.
But best of all, the grand finale, starring someone new:
Enigma the Incredible (and Magic Bertie, too)!

That evening, heading homeward in the hush that nighttime brings,
A grandpa and his grandson talked of wild and wondrous things.
For magic doesn't lie in wands or funny hats to wear.
It only takes someone to dream, and someone else to share.

They journeyed on through mystic realms, as Great Magicians should.
"Come visit soon . . ." old Grandpa said.

And Bertie said he would.

The End

Dear Magicians,

Enigma wrote a list of where he hid all the magic items—then he forgot how to decode it. Poor Enigma! Here are the missing magical things—see if you can find them.

Babushka Doll	Jar of Crackers	Magic Wand
Queen of Hearts	Jade Bells	Top Hat
Interlocking Rings	Mystic Sphinx	Silver Cape with Red Trim
Ball and Cups	Magic Rope	

While you are searching for the missing things, be sure to keep an eye out for Enigma. He is somewhere in every scene, along with lots of magic paw prints—nine in every picture.

By the way, do you know which countries my friends and I come from? See if you can discover our hometowns, too. And where do we all live now?

The key to the code that unlocks the answers to these puzzles can be found in the cabinet at the back of the book. Have fun!

Grandpa Gadzooks the Great